P9-BZJ-107

There's a Skeleton Inside You!

IDAN BEN-BARAK and JULIAN FROST

ROARING BROOK PRESS
New York

Quog and Oort are on their way to
Kevin's birthday party.

Unfortunately, there's been a slight detour.

Cherry Tree Elementary
Media Center
Carmel, IN 46033

Text copyright © 2020 by Idan Ben-Barak and Julian Frost
Illustrations copyright © 2020 by Julian Frost
Published by Roaring Brook Press
Roaring Brook Press is a division of Holtzbrinck Publishing Holdings Limited Partnership
120 Broadway, New York, NY 10271
mackids.com
All rights reserved

Library of Congress Cataloging-in-Publication Data is available.

ISBN 978-1-250-17537-3

Our books may be purchased in bulk for promotional, educational, or business use.
Please contact your local bookseller or the Macmillan Corporate and Premium Sales Department
at (800) 221-7945 ext. 5442 or by email at MacmillanSpecialMarkets@macmillan.com.

First published in Australia in 2020 by Allen & Unwin
First American edition, 2020

Book design by Monique Sterling

Printed in China by Hung Hing Off-set Printing Co., Ltd.
Heshan City Guangdong Province

1 3 5 7 9 10 8 6 4 2

DON'T WORRY, OORT, I'LL FIX THE SHIP AND WE'LL BE ON OUR WAY IN NO TIME! JUST AS SOON AS YOU OPEN THE DOOR.
I CAN'T OPEN DOORS. I'M A GAS CLOUD.

It looks like they're
going to need a hand.

Turn the page to help Quog and Oort open the spaceship door.

Give Quog and Oort a wave.

WOW, YOU HAVE HANDS!
I THINK HANDS MIGHT BE USEFUL FOR FIXING THE SPACESHIP.

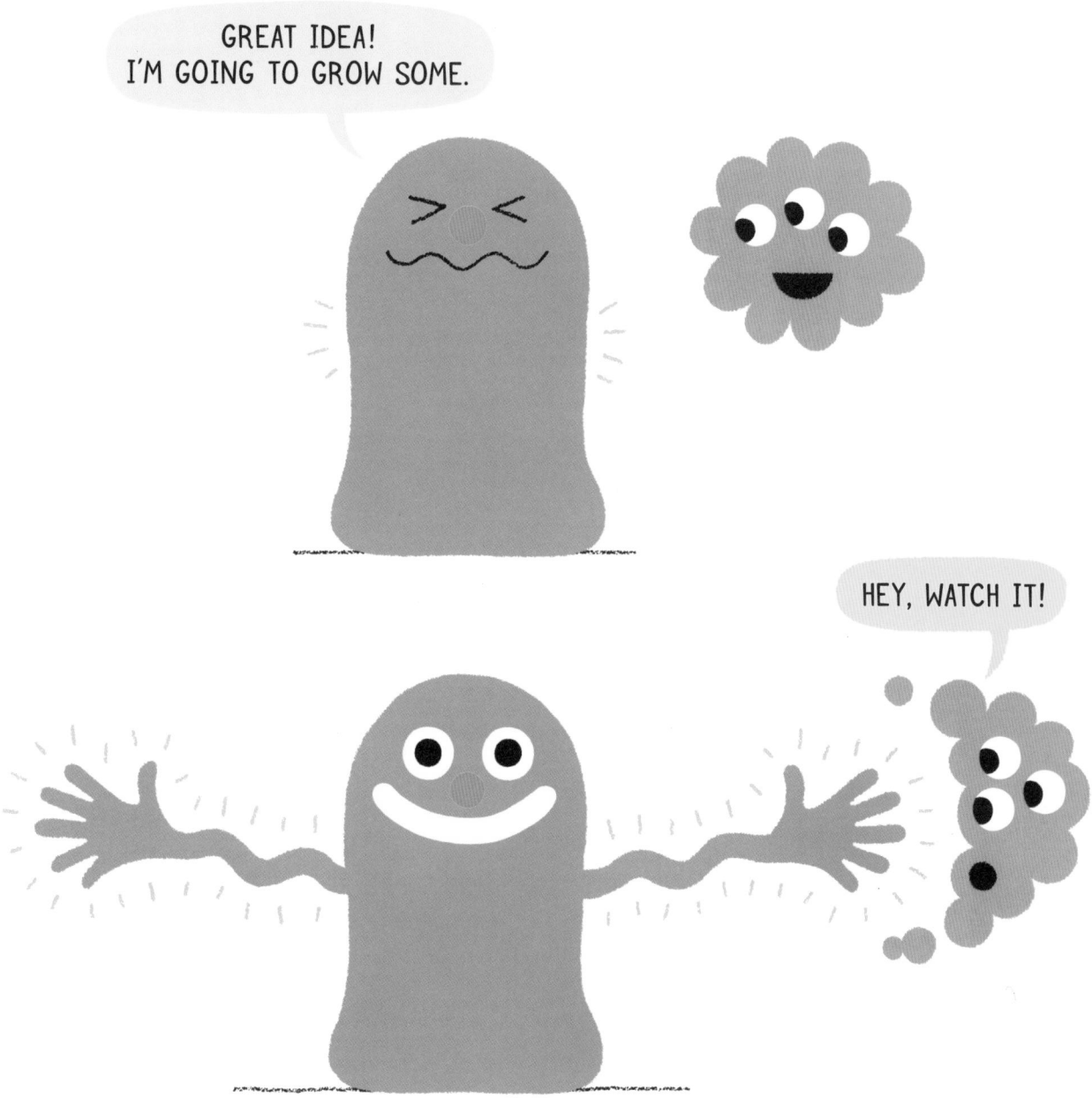

Now it's time for Quog to fix the ship so they can get to the party.

First, Quog needs to push the engine down the hill with her new hands.

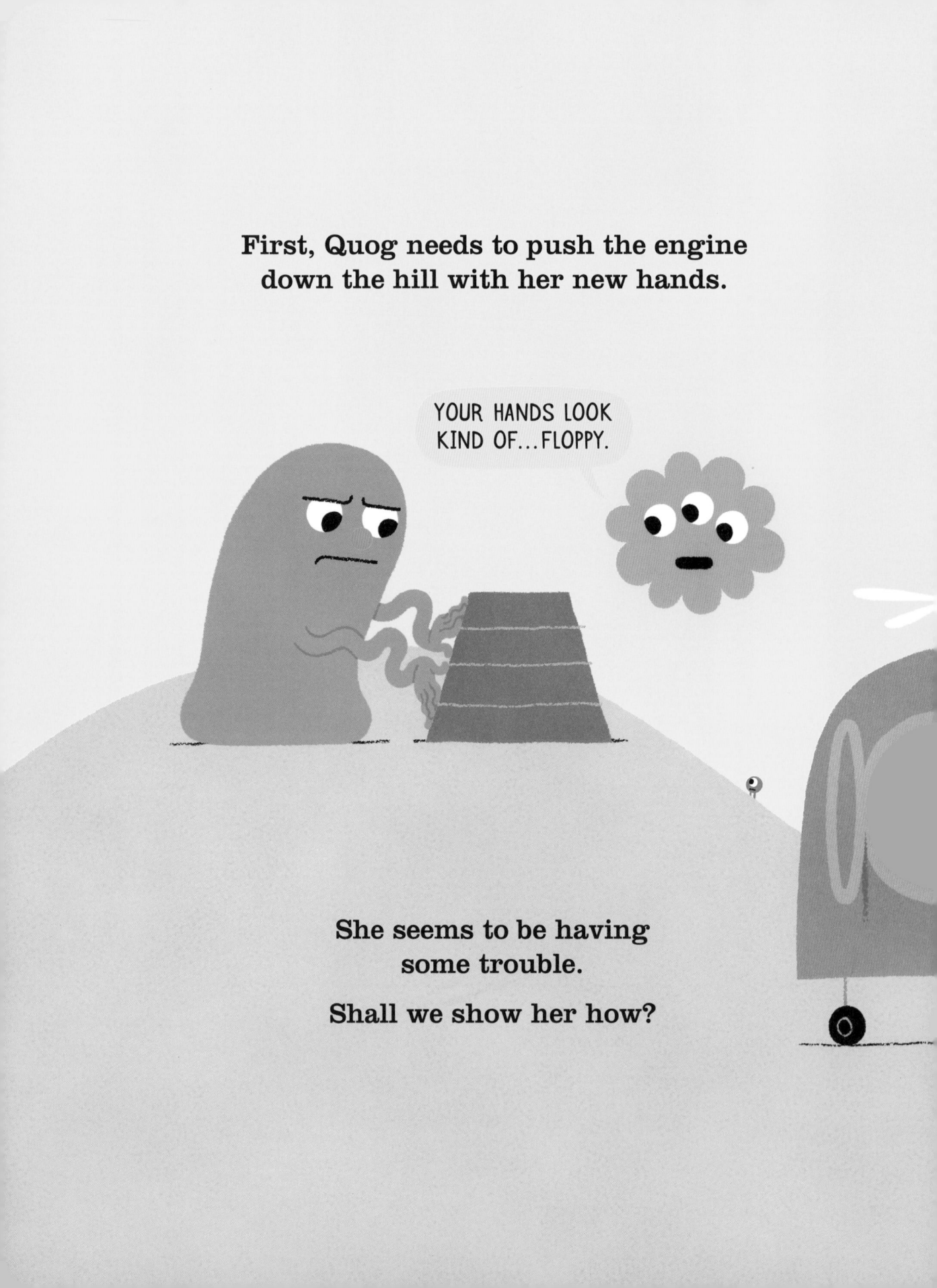

She seems to be having some trouble.

Shall we show her how?

Give the page a push right here:

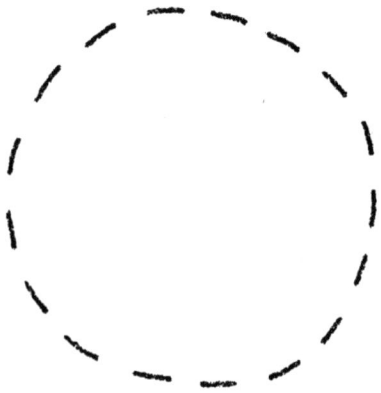

Let's show Quog and Oort what's inside your hands that keeps them straight.

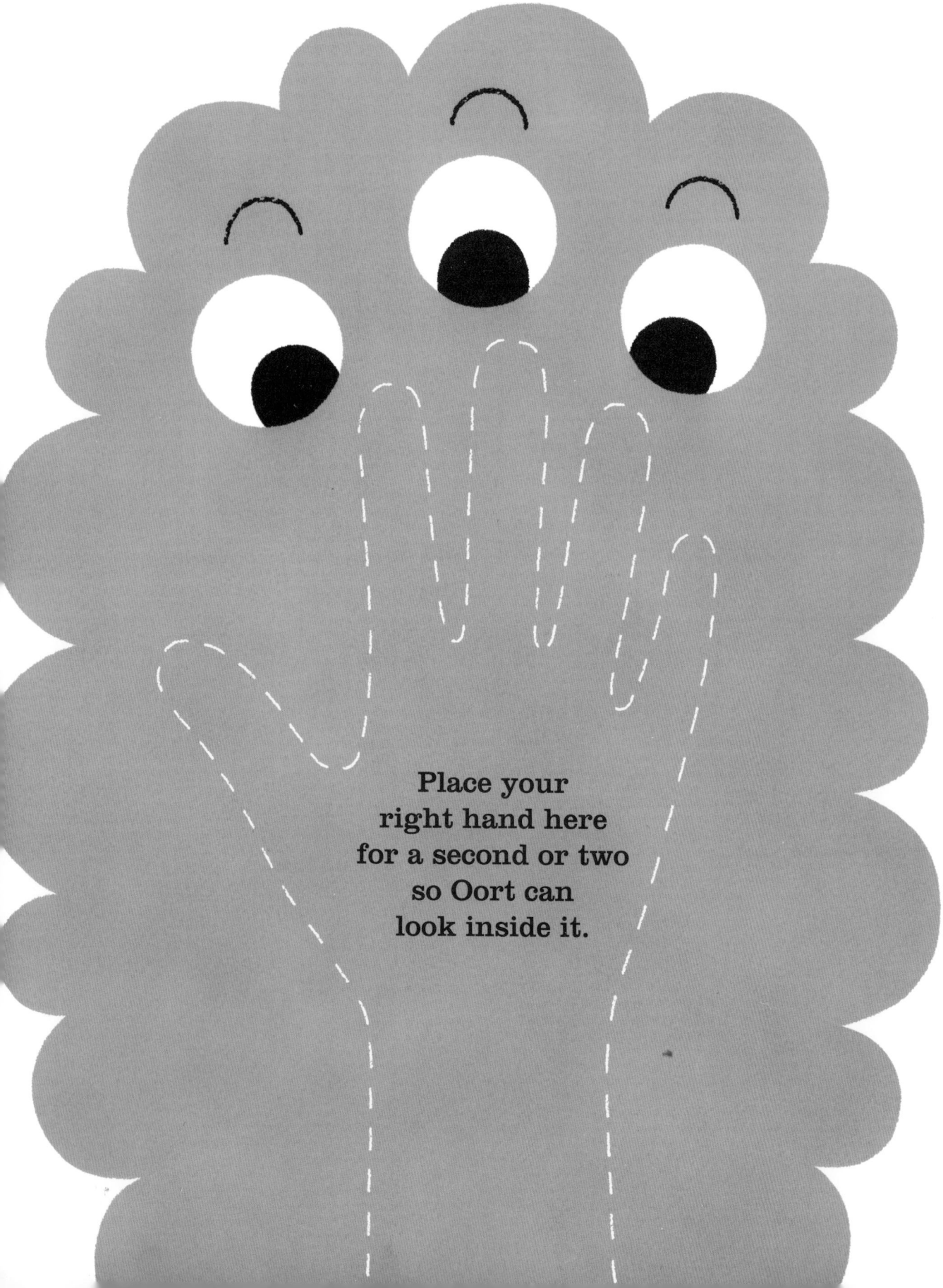
Place your
right hand here
for a second or two
so Oort can
look inside it.

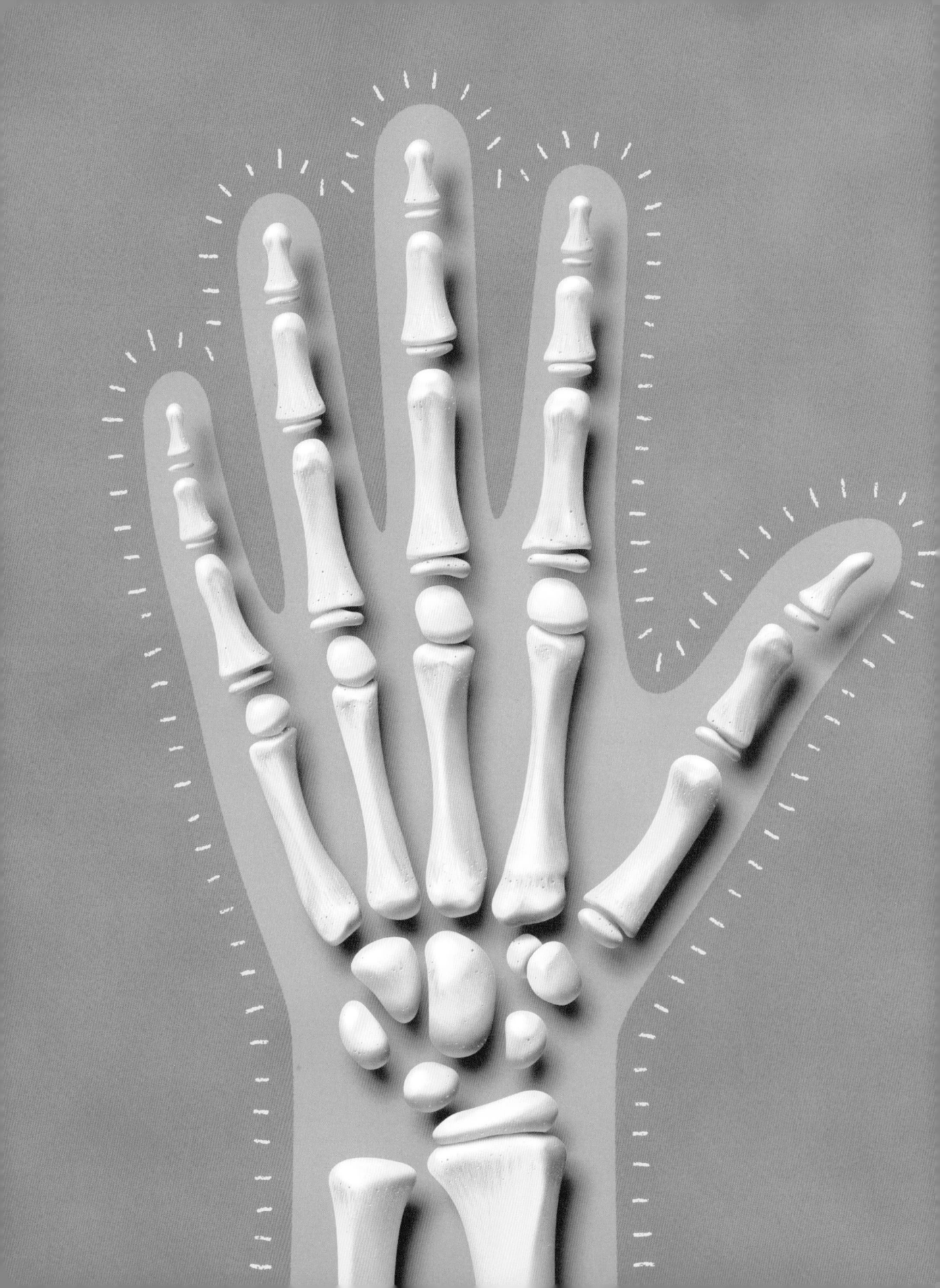

Those are your bones.
They keep your body nice and straight.

Bones give your body structure and help you move.
Without bones you'd be like jelly.

Now Quog needs to lift the engine into place.

She seems to be having some trouble.

Shall we show her how?

Lift this book up above your head.

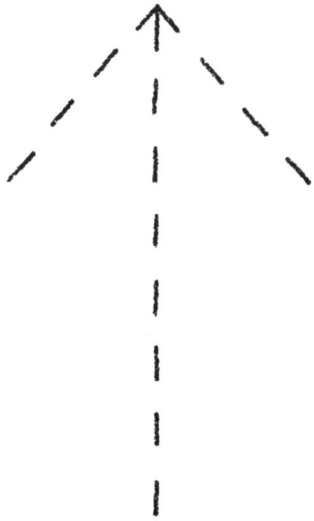

Let's show Quog and Oort what's inside your hands that makes them strong.

Place your
hand here so Oort
can look inside.

Gently now.

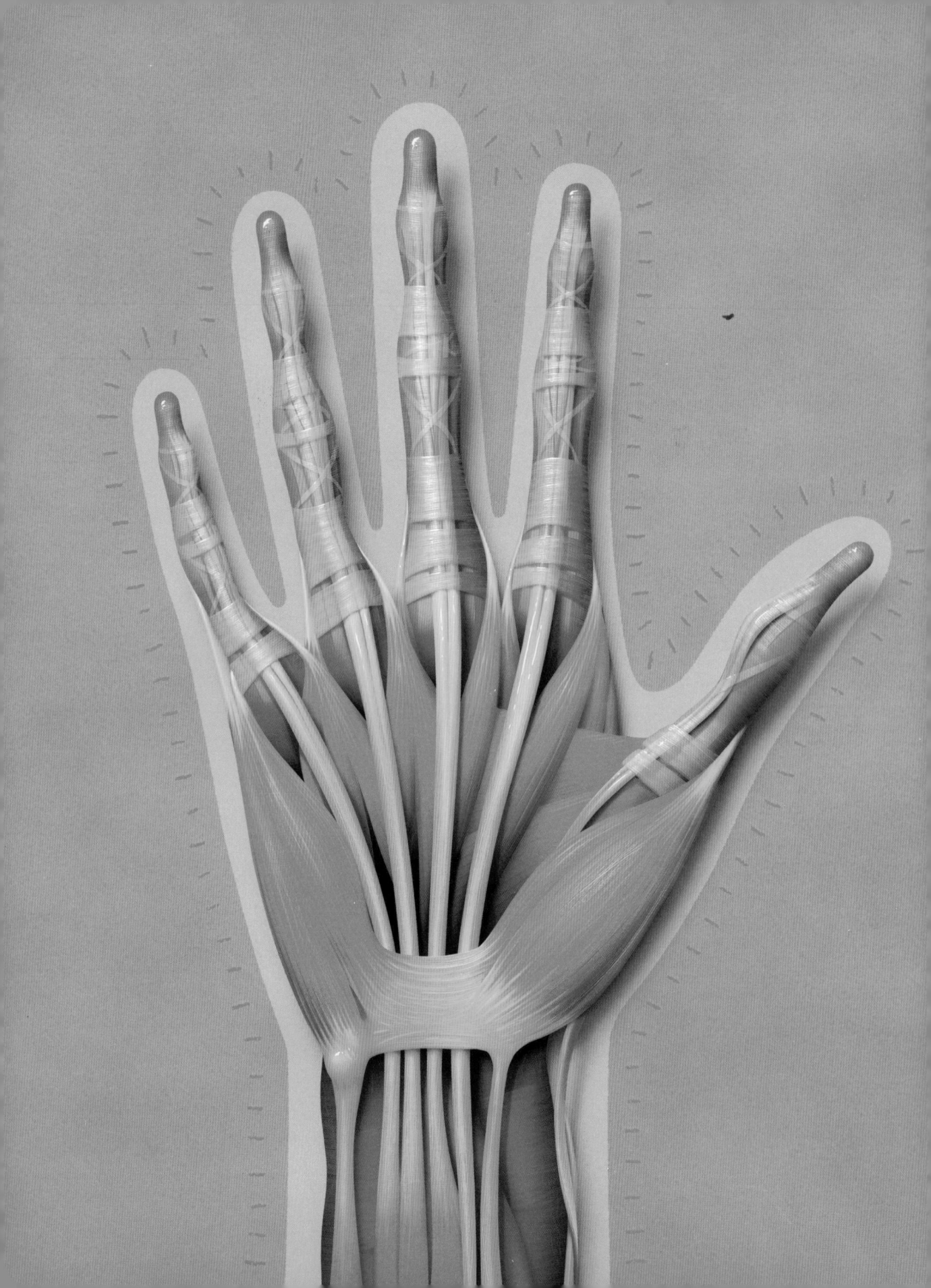

Those are your muscles.
They give you strength to do stuff.

Muscles connect to your bones. When they contract they pull the bones and make you move.

The final thing Quog needs to do is turn the ship's power back on.

Quog seems to be having trouble feeling with her hands in the dark.

Shall we show her how?

Close your eyes, then turn
the page without looking.

Let's show Quog and Oort what's inside your hand that lets it feel things.

Place your
hand here so Oort
can look inside.

It might tingle a bit.

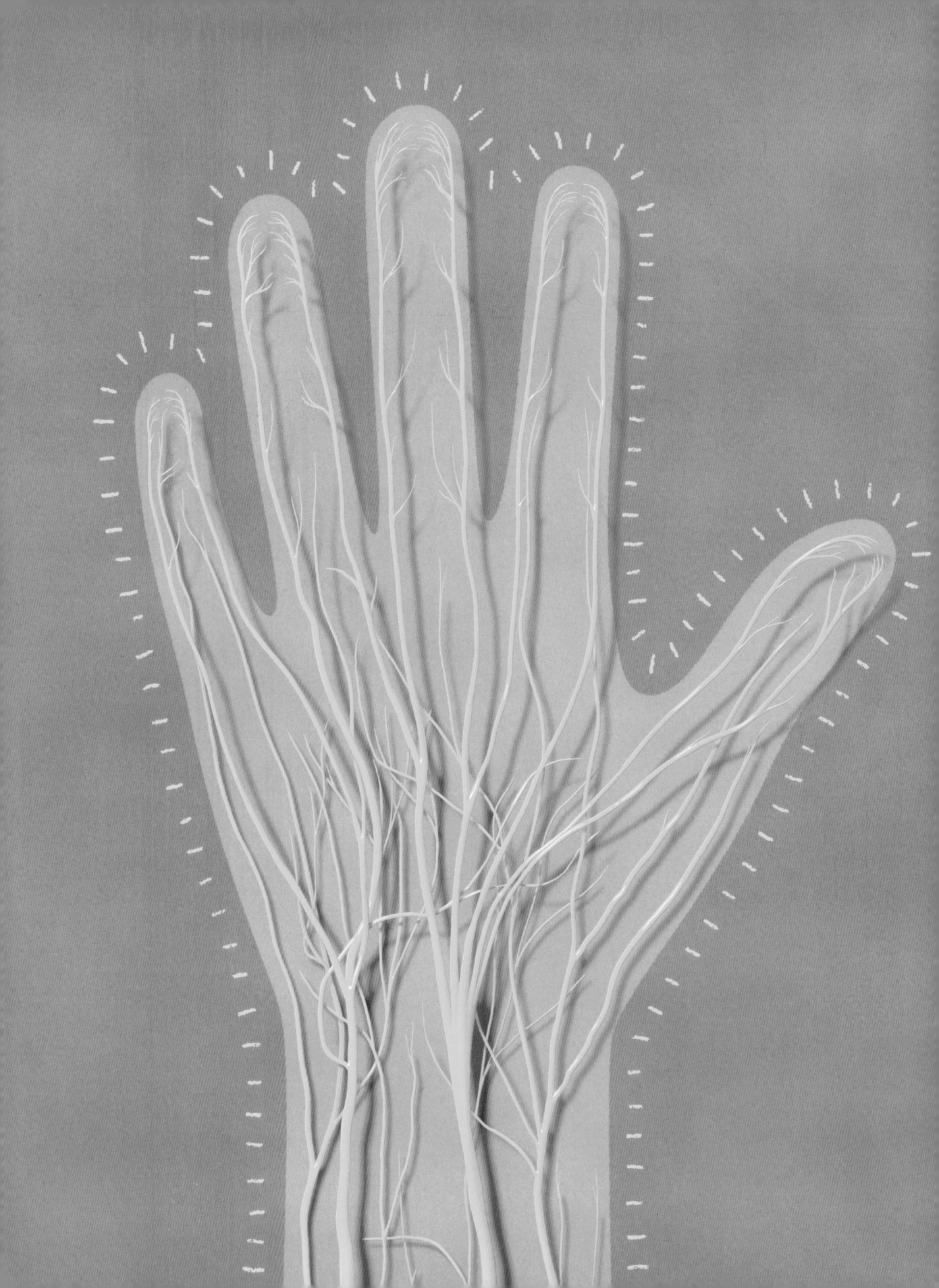

Those are your nerves. They let your hands feel what you're touching.

Nerves send messages to your brain, telling it about things like shape, textures, and temperature.

The engine is attached to the spaceship, the power is on, and Quog and Oort are ready to blast off to Kevin's birthday party.

GIVE ME A HIGH FIVE!

Away they go!

HEY, QUOG, WHAT SHALL WE GIVE KEVIN FOR HIS BIRTHDAY?
I HAVE AN IDEA.

How to grow hands

Quog seems very happy with her new alien hands. Now that you've seen how it's done, maybe you'd like to grow some more hands yourself! Extra hands are always useful.

Here's how to put your bones, muscles, and nerves together:

1 First, connect your bones to your muscles.
Then connect your muscles to your brain with nerves:

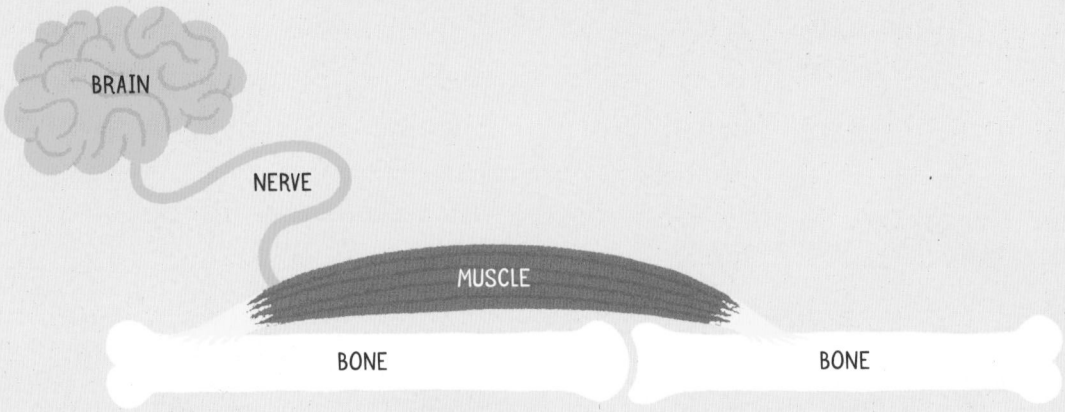

2 Now that your nerves are connected, they send electrical signals from your hand to your brain about what your hand is feeling. The brain can also send signals back through the nerves to your hand, telling it to move:

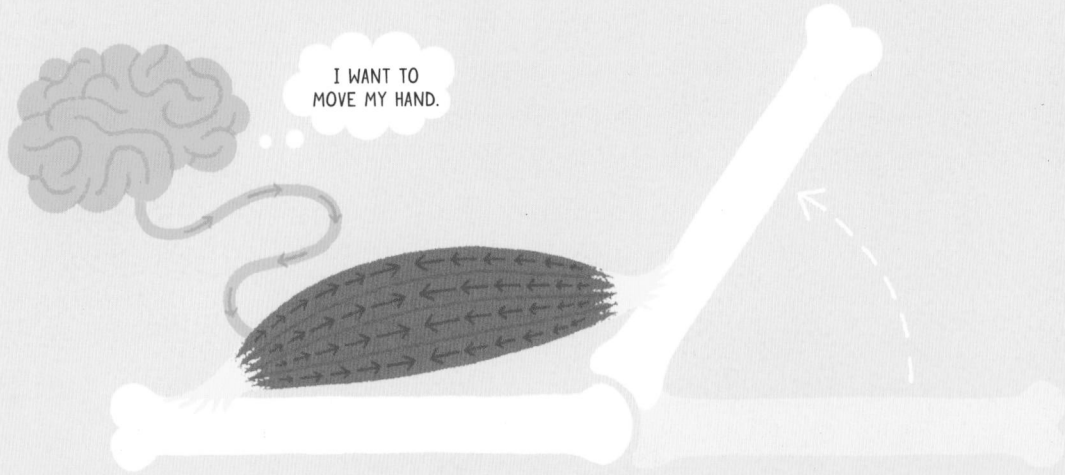

A muscle receives the signal and contracts, which pulls the bone it's attached to. Ta-da! Your hand moves.

Cherry Tree Elementary
Media Center
Carmel, IN 46033